To Taj, a sweet little monster

All rights reserved. Published in the United States by Schwartz & Wade Books, an imprint of Random House
Children's Books, a division of Penguin Random House LLC, New York.

Schwartz & Wade Books and the colophon are trademarks of Penguin Random House LLC.

Visit us on the Web! randomhousekids.com

Educators and librarians, for a variety of teaching tools, visit us at RHTeachersLibrarians.com

Library of Congress Cataloging-in-Publication Data is available upon request.
ISBN 978-1-5247-0175-8 (hc) — ISBN 978-1-5247-0176-5 (lib. bdg.)
ISBN 978-1-5247-0177-2 (ebook)

The text of this book is set in Bodoni Old Face.
The illustrations were rendered in oil paint, acrylic paint, and colored pencil.

MANUFACTURED IN CHINA
2 4 6 8 10 9 7 5 3 1
First Edition

Duck & Goose
Honk! Quack!

BOO!

by Tad Hills

schwartz & wade books · new york

Duck and Goose sat watching as day slowly became evening.
"So, Goose, what are you going to be tomorrow?" Duck asked.

Goose hesitated. "*Be?* Tomorrow? Well, I think I will be myself, Duck. It's important to always be yourself."

"Very true, Goose, except for *tomorrow*. Tomorrow is Halloween! It's the day *not* to be yourself!"

Suddenly, out of nowhere, Thistle appeared.
"Did someone say *Halloween*? I love Halloween! I'm not telling what my costume is. It's a secret," she quacked. As she sped off into the shadows, she called, "See you tomorrow. And beware the swamp monster!"

Goose gulped. "*Swamp monster?* Why would she say 'Beware the swamp monster'?"

"Hmmm. Maybe the swamp monster comes out on Halloween," Duck quacked.

"Duck, I am not a fan of monsters."

"I don't like monsters, either, Goose. But I do like trick-or-treating!"

Later that night, Goose tried not to think about the swamp monster. A shiver ran up his spine as he watched clouds creep across the moon like ghosts. His beak quaked as he listened to the groaning wind rattle the branches.

Duck closed his eyes and thought of a bag full of treats.

The next day was Halloween.
Duck got ready to go trick-or-treating.

So did Goose.

Meanwhile, Thistle was getting ready, too.

While Goose waited for Duck, he spotted a scary ghost coming toward him.

"Hello, Goose!" the ghost called. "Are you ready to go trick-or-treating?"

"Who are you?!" Goose honked.

"It's me. . . . Duck."

"You look more like a ghost to me," Goose honked. "How do I know you're not a ghost?"

"I'm not *really* a ghost," Duck quacked. "Look at my feet."

Goose had to admit no one had feet like Duck. "I'd recognize those feet anywhere," he honked.

"Then let's go!" Duck quacked.

"Do you think we'll see a swamp monster tonight?" Goose asked nervously. "I hope not," Duck quacked. "I hope we see lots of treats!"

When they reached the edge of the forest, trick-or-treating had already begun. Goose sighed with relief. No monsters in sight.

"Hello down there!" called a squirrel. "I see a spooky ghost and a brave superhero."

"Actually, these are costumes. We are Duck and Goose," honked Goose.

"Trick or treat!" quacked Duck.

"Excuse me," said a friendly daisy. "Did you say you are Duck and Goose? I just met a swamp monster who's looking for you."

Goose froze. "A SWAMP MONSTER?" he asked.
"Duck, why would a swamp monster be looking for *us*?"
"I don't know, Goose. And I don't want to know."

"Oh, there's the swamp
monster now," said the friendly
daisy. "And it's heading this way."

Duck and Goose turned and saw the scariest, slimiest, and
most hideous swamp monster EVER.

"It's after us! Run, Duck, run!" cried Goose.

Duck and Goose took cover.

They huddled together and were as quiet as they could be. They heard the *thump*, *thump*, *thump* of the swamp monster's footsteps getting closer and closer.

"Oh, Duck," Goose groaned. "We're goners!"

The footsteps suddenly stopped.

"Duck? Goose? Is that you?"
the swamp monster called.

"You're right, Goose," Duck whispered. "We're doomed!"

Suddenly, Goose remembered his cape and the G on his chest.
"Duck, I am a brave superhero. And you are the spookiest
ghost I've ever seen! And there are two of us and only one swamp
monster," Goose whispered. "We can scare it away!"

And with that, the brave superhero and the spooky ghost leapt out from behind the leafy bush. Goose honked his bravest honk and Duck quacked his scariest quack.

"BOO!"

they hollered together.

"Yikes! You sure scared me!" the swamp monster quacked.
"I've been looking everywhere for you!"
"*Thistle?*" Goose honked.
"Is that you?" Duck quacked.

"How do you like my costume?" asked Thistle. "I told you to beware the swamp monster. Pretty scary, aren't I?"

"I've seen scarier," Duck quacked.

"We don't scare easily," Goose added.

"Well, that's good, because it's time to go trick-or-treating," Thistle quacked.

And so the ghost, the brave superhero, and the scariest, slimiest, most hideous swamp monster ever wandered the forest, filling their bags with Halloween treats.

Later, back in the meadow, Duck and Goose sorted through their treats. In the light of the moon, they shared Halloween stories about a masked superhero, a spooky ghost, and a swamp monster who wasn't really that scary after all.